Blade RUNNER, a MOVie

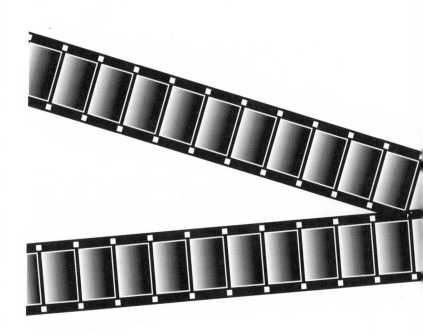

WILLIAM S. BURROUGHS

BIade RUnneR, a MOViE

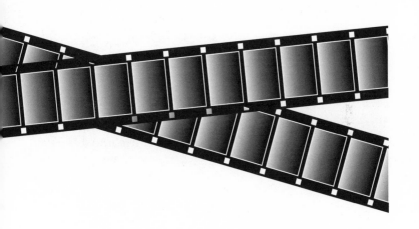

bLUe wiNd PREss
BERkeLey 1999

The author wishes to thank Alan E. Nourse, upon whose book, *The Blade Runner,* characters and situations in this book are based.

LIBRARY OF CONGRESS CATALOGING IN PUBLICATION DATA:

Burroughs, William S.   1914 – 1997
    Blade runner: a movie

    I. Title.

PZ4.B972B1   [PS3552.U75]   813'.5'4   78-21584
ISBN 0-912652-45-4   CLOTH (OUT OF PRINT)
ISBN 0-912652-46-2   PAPERBACK
ISBN 0-912652-47-0   LIMITED SIGNED EDITION (OUT OF PRINT)

Book Design and cover collage © Copyright 1986 by George Mattingly. This Fifth Printing of the Second Edition was manufactured in spring 1999 for Blue Wind Press, 820 Miramar Avenue, Berkeley, California 94707 by Thomson-Shore, INC., Dexter, Michigan.

99 00 01 02 03 04 9 8 7 6 5

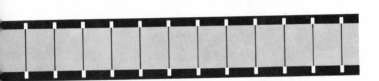

Now B.J. you are asking me to tell you in one sentence what this film is about? I'm telling you it is too big for one sentence—even a life sentence. For starters it's about the National Health Insurance we don't got. It's about plain middle-class middle-income-bracket Joe, the $15,000-a-year boy, sweating out two jobs, I.R.S. wringing the moonlight dollars out of him to keep the niggers and the spics on welfare and medicare so they can keep up their strength to mug his grandmother, rape his sister, and bugger his ten-year-old son. How much money does 15G Joe have in the bank after I.R.S. hits him for the service?

Less than nothing. Can he afford to pay $300 a day for a hospital bed?

Pushers on welfare and medicare lean out of a Mercedes and spit in his face…. "IS THIS WHAT I PAY TAXES FOR?"

"We gotta be careful of ethnic slurs."

"Well it's the way some folks feel. Part of the whole picture. Fascism is defeated in the end by the American dream."

This film is about overpopulation and the growth of vast service bureaucracies. The FDA and AMA and the big drug companies are like an octopus on the citizen. You're dying of cancer, see? The doctor gives you no hope, wants you out of his office as quick as possible because you don't carry health insurance or qualify for medicare. All he gives you is a grudging RX for darvon. Any croaker gives a dying cancer patient darvon should be broken down to bedpan duty in an animal hospital.

So you wanta do something about your big C. You've heard about laetrile, Reich's orgone accumulators, a doctor in France with a magnetic machine, another French doctor who has cured cancer with inoculations of Chagas' disease, and someone in Rumania…. Can you even try these remedies? Fuck no. The FDA won't let them on the market—they even destroyed Reich's *writings.* Now who is to decide whether I take laetrile or use an orgone accumulator for my terminal cancer? Me or the FDA? After all it's me that's dying.

Is this freedom? Is this what America stands for?

So America goes underground. They all make their own medicines in garages, basements, and lofts, and provide their own service. This manual is in every pocket: YOU DON'T NEED A DOCTOR. All the kids learn to give injections in school. You don't need a doctor for such simple complaints as leprosy, syphilis, typhoid fever, malaria, dysentery. All you need is access to the medications.

To alleviate the pain and discomfort of these and other complaints, salutary draughts of laudanum should be administered at eight-hour intervals, supplemented by supportive injections of morphine if any residual unease remains outstanding, since the euphoria and relief afforded by an adequate dosage of opiates is one of the solaces of illness. No medicine chest should be without God's Own Medicine. Mom wears the key around her neck. There she is, reaching for it on a *Saturday Evening Post* cover.

This film is about America. What America was and what America could be, and how those who try to stifle the American dream are defeated. We have been taught that if you put a better product on the free market, the superior product will sell. So you got the seven-year Amazon Pill and a loft lab. Are you going to get the OK from the FDA to put the big drug combines off the Pill market? You should live so long. In this film we don't need their OK. Medicine has gone underground. And underground medicine saves the world from disaster.

This film is about cancer and that's a powerful subject. Already doctors are talking about an epidemic. In the film a strain of epidemic flash-cancer is stopped by virus B-23, a virus of biologic mutation which restores humanity to pristine health.

This film is about a city we all know and love, a city which has come to represent all cities. In the year 2014 New York, world center for underground medicine, is the most glamorous, the most dangerous, the most exotic, vital, far-out city the world has ever seen. The only public transport is the old IRT limping along at five miles an hour through dimly-lit tunnels. The other lines are derelict. Hand-propelled and steam-driven cars transport produce, the stations have been converted into markets. The lower tunnels are flooded, giving rise to an underground Venice.

The upper reaches of derelict skyscrapers, without elevator service since the riots, have been taken over by hang-glider and autogyro gangs, mountaineers and steeple-jacks. A sky boy steps off his penthouse into a parachute on guide wires that drop him to a street-level landing. The parachute is retracted by hand-operated winches and pulleys, or a delco motor. (The sky boys compete with the subs for control of electrical service in the lower city.) Or the sky boy may use wire slides with a jump seat under the carriage, zig-zagging down from landing platform to landing platform. Or he may skip from roof to roof in his hang-glider, or use his autogyro parachute. Buildings are joined by suspension bridges, a maze of platforms, catwalks, slides, lifts. Inside these buildings, light elevators that can carry several hundred pounds have been installed.

During the 1984 riots some jokers dumped all the fish from the aquariums, all the reptiles and amphibians, into the waterways of New York—and now freshwater sharks cruise the Hudson. Water boas, alligators, piranha fish, electric eels, infest the subway tunnels, the swamps and canals, sometimes materializing in swimming pools, bathtubs, and toilet bowls. All the zoo animals were also released—and killer bears now roam Central Park. The man-eating leopard on Third Avenue was finally shot from a tree surgeon's rig, with a half-eaten faggot as bait. Other species have settled down to co-exist, the jackals, wolves, foxes and hyenas mating with the vast wild dog packs.

This is the background against which the film revolves. Any treatment, any drug, any vice can be found here for a price.

This film is about a second chance for Billy the blade runner, and for all humanity. For the virus makes a hole in time, and Billy steps into the past—which is also the future.

This film is about the future of medicine and the future of man. For man *has* no future unless he can throw off the dead past and absorb the underground of his own being. In the end, underground medicine merges with the medical establishment, to the great benefit of both. The large number of trained practitioners who are not licensed doctors takes a vast burden off the profession, drastically reducing the price of medical care. Experimental drugs and treatments now have access to all the equipment and resources of modern laboratories. Doctors learn, in addition to Western medicine: acupuncture, osteopathy, herbal remedies, and all methods of Eastern healing. New branches of medicine evolve. Prophylactic medicine... "If you get sick, I pay you." Pros are taught to consider the patient as a functioning organism in relation to his entire environment. To what illness would such an organism be subject? How can such illnesses be averted many years before they develop? Far from being computerized, diagnosis becomes a fine art. Some can diagnose a case entirely by the sense of smell.

The doctor sniffs. He shakes his head with a terrible smile.

"I am referring your case to the coroner."

Others rely on disease-sniffing dogs. The dog sniffs, then throws back its head and howls. The dog bares its teeth and growls ominously at an incipient tumor.

Young and attractive doctors use sexual contact as a

means of diagnosis. Kirilian photography, voice-print and handwriting analysis are standard procedures.

Now here are a few sample shots.

He riffles through stills from the movie like a deck of cards....

Scene is lower Manhattan, 2014. Poses problem as to how background material is to be presented on screen. Postulate a story set in the 1960's, written by an omniscient writer in the 1930's. Writer knows about World War II, the atom bomb, Vietnam, the drug problem, inflation, rock stars, gay lib, women's lib, the Black Panthers. How, in terms of what is actually presented on screen, can we acquaint those living in the 1930's with a 1960 background, with what is common knowledge to anyone living in the 1960's? Of course, someone can give a brief summary of the milestones which separate the world of the audience from the world on the screen; but this is an awkward expedient. Such a narrator constitutes a stilted and improbable device.

How can the background be shown solely in terms

of what people say, experience, and do on screen? World War II movie on TV, man pays $3 for a haircut, TV program on the atom bomb 20 years after, dishwasher picks up check for $90 for a week's work, narcs arrest pop star, Vietnam on TV, demonstrations, memory flash-backs. Audience gets the picture in bits and pieces.

So here is the background for 1999 presented as narrative....

Helicopter view of Manhattan...

"Overpopulation has led to ever-increasing governmental control over the private citizen, not on the old-style police-state models of oppression and terror, but in terms of work, credit, housing, retirement benefits, and medical-care: services that can be withheld. These services are computerized. No number, no service. However, this has not produced the brainwashed standardized human units postulated by such linear prophets as George Orwell. Instead, a large percentage of the population has been forced underground. How large, no one knows. These people are *numberless*."

Newborn babies howl. Subdivisions, housing projects grow. Computers buzz in Con Ed, I.R.S., Welfare, Medicare, Health Insurance. Forms, notices, bills pour out.

Exasperated citizen packs one suitcase and walks out of his Levittown house. He rakes some leaves together, dumps a stack of forms on top, and sets the heap on fire. Old woman across the street rushes to the phone. Squad car arrives and gives him a summons for burning leaves. As the squad car drives away he drops the summons into the ashes. He walks away with his suitcase.

Aerial view of the Wall that runs along 23rd Street to the Hudson and the East River...

"The Wall was built after the Health Act Riot of 1984. The Lower City can be cut off and the wall manned with troops on half an hour's notice. A similar wall cuts Harlem off from central Manhattan...."

The helicopter moves south... rubble, ruined buildings, vacant lots. It looks like London after The Blitz. Few signs of reconstruction, except for sporadic patchwork. Many streets are blocked with refuse and obviously impassable. Here and there, shabby open-air markets and vegetable gardens in vacant lots. Some are crowded, others virtually deserted. Crowded squares and streets abruptly empty for no apparent reason. There are improvised boats on the rivers, loaded with produce.

"By 1980, pressure had been growing to put through a National Health Act. This was blocked by the medical lobby, doctors protesting that such an Act would mean the virtual end of private practice, and that the overall quality of medical service would decline. The strain on an already precarious economy was also cited. Drug companies, fearing that price regulation would slash profits, spent millions to lobby against the proposed bill and ran full-page ads in all the leading newspapers. And above all, the health insurance companies screamed that the Act was unnecessary and could only lead to increased taxes for inferior service.

Here is the middle-income-bracket citizen in his rundown apartment. The roof leaks and he has been trying for weeks to get it fixed. The landlord does nothing. The citizen has just shared a tin of dog food with his family.

"Here we are, paying to keep the niggers and the spics and the beatniks in hotels and hospitals. We pay for their stinking dope habits, give them money not to work, and *what about us?* Can we afford to spend $500 a day for a hospital bed?

They find a spokesman in the Reverend Parcival, who puts out a paper known as *The Watchdog,* with a cartoon strip:

Blond Nordic couple carry sick child to a hospital. A black doctor throws them into the street:

"Unqualified filth."

He welcomes a Puerto Rican youth who has skinned his knuckle in a brawl.

"Come right in my boy. Nurse, quarter grain G.O.M. for this gentleman."

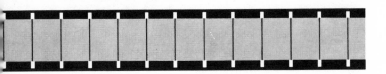

"Heroin was legalized for addicts in 1980. The United States Health Service took over distribution through government clinics and built up an intricate bureaucracy, with police and investigators who turned out to be totally corrupt. Many people who were not addicts got on the program and made a comfortable living selling off their allowance."

Here is Mr. Middle Income again. He has a painful and disabling case of shingles. He has just paid a doctor $50 for a visit. The doctor refuses to prescribe codeine:

"Only thing I can prescribe is Whitefield's ointment."

And here is one big happy welfare family. Knock on

any Harlem door. Two boys on heroin maintenance, a daughter in the federal leprosarium at Carrville, Louisiana, one retarded in Kings State, one muscular dystrophy on a special program. Ma collects on all of them—loss of support allowance. No work, no worries. Color TV. Remains of a huge turkey on the table. Ma helps herself to a liberal dose of her own special heroin cough syrup to keep out the winter colds. Pa is eating strawberry ice cream. The kids sprawl on the floor studying travel folders. They can't decide whether to go to Lexington for the summer cure ("The Country Club" now earns its moniker with miles of woodlands, hiking, horses, golf, tennis, boating, and fishing available to inmates), or to visit Sis in Carrville.

"My God," Pa groans, "I got an ice cream headache. Give me a shot, son, quick... it's going away...."

Doctor hands boy his heroin script with a corrupt leer....

"Now don't let me *catch you* selling any off the top."

He picks up the phone. "Nurse, how many lepers out there bucking for Carrville?"

The traffic in Hansen's bacillus is rampant. It's now known as "the white stuff." Just scratch a patch of skin with a needle and rub it on, and six months later....

New lepers stream out of an old paddle-wheel riverboat singing "Home Sweet Home". Others drop off at lonely sidings, frogs croaking....

"Welcome to the Hansen family. You'll just have to imagine my hand...never bounce me off the program. They can arrest you, and return you to civilian life if you aren't careful. Now I handle the best white stuff in Carrville. Stay on the program with Doc White's Ointment."

Along the bayous, lakes, and rivers are the cottages covered with bougainvillea, roses and morning glories, where the languid lepers lounge—smoking pot and opium from their gardens, shooting government H, oranges mangoes and avocados growing in the backyard, catching catfish bass and perch from the front porch, or opening tins from the government store.

Carrville is now a huge area of swampland, stretching from the Great Thicket of East Texas to the Everglades of Florida. On swamp islands strange rites are celebrated. Naked youths with alligator masks dance before the Gator Goat God who has the head of an alligator and the feet of a goat.

Mardi Gras time in Carrville. A languid young aristocrat drifts by on a flower float, one leg eaten off at the knee, the stump phosphorescent in the gathering dusk.

A radioactive strain my dear, terribly chic. Violet lagoons where fishes of emerald dive for the moon. And here is a stunning young leper in Cleopatra drag on her barge with a dishy Marc Antony....

And the whole reservation is fenced and guarded.

"So we leave the happy people of Carrville, who, through some inner source of courage and strength, have turned their terrible affliction into a rewarding way of life."

"Is this what I pay taxes for? Queer sex orgies and injections of marijuana?"

"In our splendid facilities—provided by the kind American government—we do not have to concern ourselves with assholes like you who work for a living. May you prolapse into the privy from which you emerged."

Mafiosos lean out of their Cadillacs to spit in the taxpayer's face.

"Who you, worka fora living? I speet in your crumb face."

And many youths claimed disability, saying they could not co-exist with disgusting taxpaying slobs.

"They make me so nervous I have been unable to work. I claim full disability and heroin maintenance."

"When the third National Health Act was defeated in the Senate as a result of shameless lobbying and obstructive tactics, the Health Act Riots of 1984 broke out. It is estimated that 500,000 people died in New York City alone, and property damage was in the billions. Other cities counted comparable casualties. The total fatalities throughout the U.S. ran close to ten million.

Ironically, the high death rate was largely due to the government's efforts to forestall the outbreak by strict weapon-control measures. The National Firearms Registration Act of 1982 debarred anyone with a criminal record or any record of drug addiction or mental illness, and all those on the welfare rolls, from buying or possessing any firearms of any description including air guns. This left the disaffected middle-class in possession of more firearms than any other group.

"Relying on stockpiled weapons and the sympathy of the police and the National Guard, Parcival's Soldiers of Christ now talked openly of taking over New York and slaughtering all ethnic minorities, beatniks, dope fiends, queers and longhairs. In fact they talked too much and scared too many people, dropping dark hints about international bankers and Wall Street and the Yellow Peril. Did this mean the Jews, the wealthy and the Chinese were also on the list? Powerful anonymous figures decided it might be prudent to provide effective opposition to Parcival's followers. In any case a document known as *The Devil's Diary* leaked out to the minorities most immediately and specifically threatened.

"*The Devil's Diary* had been prepared on orders from the CIA in the 1960's. It contained detailed instructions for assembling weapons from materials easily available in any grocery or hardware store: black powder, fire bombs, plus a battery of biological and chemical weapons. How to make botulism from canned bouillon; how to make nerve gas from bug sprays; how to make chlorine, nitroglycerine, phosgene, nitric oxide, arsenical gas. It was these weapons, delivered and supplemented by crossbows, blowguns, slingshots, and black powder grenades, that occasioned the staggering casualties."

August 6, 1984...Parcival's Soldiers of Christ have gathered in Central Park. Unopposed by the police, they now split into two columns marching north and south. A series of paintings like *Custer's Last Stand* record the ensuing battles:

The Siege of St. Vincent's at 12th Street

Doctors nurses and orderlies fight the rioters with scalpels saws and bedpans. Ether bomb explodes in a corridor, stopping the rioters long enough so a doctor can pass patients down a laundry chute to safety. The hospital is on fire. A Chinese orderly throws copper into a vat of nitric acid, releasing nitric oxide. This is a delayed-action poison. Rioters who inhale the fumes collapse an hour or two later.

The March to The Sea

The Soldiers advance on the Village. Marshals are evacuating the area, concentrating their forces in the lofts and warehouses and derelict buildings of lower Manhattan. A number of gay bookstores, art galleries, and liquor stores are booby-trapped with nitric oxide, arsine, phosgene, and botulism. Blood-mad and frustrated at not finding the victims they had anticipated, the Soldiers charge into the area below 8th Street, many of them dying on their feet from various poisons they have absorbed.

Cobble stones from roof tops . . . The Soldiers of Christ rush into buildings to be met by a cloud of chlorine rolling down the stairs. Black powder grenades launched from slingshots and crossbows loaded with crushed glass and sodium cyanide. Silent blowguns with cyanide and botulism darts. By the time the Soldiers of Christ realize that the opposition is not playing fair at all, they have suffered heavy losses—and now the partisans launch hand-to-hand attacks with machetes and spears and swords. Seizing firearms from the dead and dying, they close in behind the Crusaders who, caught in a deadly crossfire and dropping from delayed action poisons, are forced into the bay, where many perish from drowning. Survivors split into small groups and, abandoning their holy crusade, take to raping, looting and killing in the middle-class neighborhoods of midtown Manhattan....

The March on Harlem General

Once again Parcival's Soldiers of Christ run into a deadly ambush of biological and chemical weapons. Punitive bands harass the white middle-class neighborhoods in Queens and the Bronx. The fighting goes on and on. Power is cut. LSD in the water supply. New York is starving. Foraging bands spread into the suburbs and the country.

Federal troops, exhaustion, starvation and disease, promises of a National Health Act and total amnesty for all rioters, finally restore order.

"Who can speak of justice with ten million Americans dead?" says the President. "We can only speak of forgetting and rebuilding."

New York looks like the aftermath of a nuclear attack. Whole areas in ruins, refugee camps, tent cities. Millions who have fled the city will not return. New York is a ghost city. Other cities are in a similar condition.

The lepers of Carrville gave a good account of themselves, fighting in swamps with improvised weapons, releasing thousands of infected armadillos, and thus gaining new converts to the ever-growing Hansen family. Carrville now extends through the swamps and timber lands of Louisiana, Mississippi, Florida, East Texas, Missouri and Arkansas. It constitutes a vast rural slum, and many non-lepers live there by preference.

The President signs the National Health Act, extending free medical care to all citizens and residents of the U.S.A. Doctors nurses and orderlies dance through hospital corridors wards and operating rooms singing

"We belong to everyone

All the best things in life are free...."

Heart monitors bleep, kidney machines gurgle, x-rays click, iron lungs wheeze....

"We belong to everyone

All the best things in life are free...."

The Health Act soon poses more problems than it solves. Drugs to halt the aging process have brought life expectancy up to 125 years, thus aggravating the population problem. On the other hand, illnesses which have seemingly been eliminated suddenly erupt in epidemic form, like the deadly adult diptheria which broke out in the late 1980's. The population, drenched with increasingly effective antibiotics, had lost all natural resistance and became as vulnerable to these infections as the Indians and South Sea Islanders on first contact with the whites.

"We run the risk of virgin soil epidemics dumping millions into our overcrowded hospitals," warns a health official.

The life span of those afflicted with hereditary degenerative illnesses like diabetes, Friedrich's ataxia, and Huntington's chorea, now enables them to reproduce well past the age of a hundred, flooding the country with recessive genes.

It was a shy, pot-smoking professor of bio-mathematics, Professor Heinz, who pointed out clearly emergent patterns: "The miracles of modern medicine, by interfering with natural immunity, in the long run give rise to more illnesses than they prevent. Those suffering from hereditary illnesses, which were formerly fatal in childhood or adolescence, can now prolong their life span indefinitely, propagating any number of defective offspring." He concluded that the planet would be inexorably flooded by the worst specimens of humanity with the lowest survival value in long-range biologic terms.

Computers checked his predictions: in another hundred years, those suffering from chronic hereditary illnesses and requiring lifelong treatment would actually be in the majority. There would not be enough healthy people left to care for them. Epidemics might well eradicate this weakened and degenerate strain. The solons were impressed, and there was talk in the House of providing incentives to voluntary sterilization for the unfit.

However, the incentives provided in the National Health Act Amendment (commonly known as *HAA*) were negative. The unfit were to be denied medical service of any kind unless they agreed to sterilization, "Unfitness" to be determined by a board of doctors and vaguely defined as "suffering from any hereditary illness, condition or tendency deemed to be biologically undesirable." Like being a nigger . . . or a wog . . . or a queer . . . or a dope fiend . . . or a psychopath . . . *HAA HAA HAA* .

The Amendment also forbade any doctor to engage in private practice, with or without remuneration, since alternative care would undermine the whole purpose of *HAA*. Protesting a genocidal white plot, thousands of blacks and Puerto Ricans burned their health cards in Central Park—and they were by no means alone. However, this massive card burning ceremony did not lead to further rioting.

Granted that Prof Heinz's conclusions were accurate, then *HAA* was completely logical: if medical care leads to further illness by reducing immunity and also keeps alive those suffering from genetic defects, it would seem reasonable to remove such individuals from the genetic pool and start reducing the population in the right areas.

When *HAA* became law in 1999, medicine went underground. A vast traffic in medical supplies sprang up, at first filled by stockpiles of medicines and instruments taken in the 1984 riots, later by hundreds of fly-by-night laboratories in lofts and basements and abandoned subway tunnels. Most doctors also carried on an illegal practice.

Lower Manhattan in 2014 has less a look of having been rebuilt than resettled. Services are limited. Only one subway line is still operating. The derelict tunnels are occupied by delco gangs, clandestine laboratories, rats and wild dogs who snarl and snap at passers-by through rusty subway grates. They are maintained by the occupants to discourage intruders. A mysterious personage known as the King of Subways has his headquarters in Queens Plaza—a dazzling construction of subway cars, change booths, turnstiles, so that part of the structure is always in motion. You get on a diner train for dinner, and get off at a northern Carrville outpost, frogs croaking in New Jersey swamps.

Vegetable gardens are everywhere—on roofs, in vacant lots and terraces and basements. Many streets are blocked with refuse since the riots. The potholes are enlarged and used as fish ponds. A reclamation project called for a series of canals across Lower Manhattan to substitute waterways for trucks, owing to the fuel shortage. The project was not completed. The canals stop in a dead-end of rusty locks and machinery. Houses along the derelict canals are sought after, though some can't get used to the damp and the mist. The fish are coming back....

Boy fishing from a concrete mixer pulls in a five-pound sea bass. He holds the fish up and pulls up to the cobblestone wharf.

"Got beeg one meester. Very good price. Twenty dollar? What you come here for? Take drug live two hundred years maybe? Plenty good monkey nuts? Whole new preeck? Too many rug rats? Here seven year Pill meester."

Lower Manhattan is a world center for underground medicine. Any drug, any operation, any treatment can be had here for a price. In this maze of tunnels, canals, abandoned buildings, lofts and basements, live all the fugitives and outlaws from the Service State. Here is Pop Street, where you can buy the brain stuff—fifty times stronger than morphine. It was thought at first to be non-addictive, but this proved to be an error. A *pop* puts the addict in a state of suspended animation, a point of almost zero metabolism from which he thaws out rotten like twice-frozen meat. He needs steady *pops* to stay frozen.

And here comes the *pop* man in his electric canoe, all black and silver to blend with the dark water and the warehouse windows . . . Needless to say, the sale or manufacture of this drug is illegal.

A flourishing black market in sperm heralds a long-range genetic war.

"Boy sperm Meester?"

Rock stars and movie actors sell off their sperm to the underground banks. Sperm trafficking is a felony, but few spermers or underground doctors are arrested and still fewer prosecuted. Obviously, the Health Inspectors are turning a blind eye and an open palm.

Lower Manhattan, 2014. Here clients come for operations, drugs, treatments, that cannot be bought for any amount of money through legal channels ... drugs suppressed by the drug manufacturers from long-range profit motives and in turn suppressed by the State bureaucracy. Apomorphine as a cure for addiction suppressed by the heroin industry and the drug enforcement agencies. Suppressed after the legalization of heroin for addicts, to keep as many addicts as possible on the program so as to maintain personnel and appropriations. Neither drug manufacturers nor the medical bureaucracy want to solve such a convenient problem.

In 1956 a contraceptive drug developed by the Amazon Indians was submitted to an American drug company for testing and eventual distribution. One dose prevents pregnancy for seven years. And one dose of another drug allows conception. Here we have a precise method of population control, at a time when overpopulation is an ever more urgent problem. Drug companies rejected the drug, since it would cut their profits. They could sell a pill a day forever, so who wanted to know about a Pill that lasts seven years? The drug was ignored from a profit motive. Subsequently outlawed by the sterilization bureaucracy, this drug is available on the underground market. Loft drug labs are not thinking in long-range terms.

The shoestring entrepreneur, the innovator, the eccentric, the adventurer, long banished to limbo by the coalition of the big drug companies and the FDA, re-appear.

Man in Amazon jungle collecting the contraceptive vine . . . basement lab . . . drug in the street . . .

"Amazon pill meester? Very good price . . . $500 . . ."

There were of course regrettable incidents, in which the wrong product was marketed. . . .

Man gargles no-cavity mouthwash and all his teeth fall out.

Sometimes standards of cleanliness and purity in the underground laboratories left much to be desired. . . .

Filthy laboratory in a former urinal, cockroaches in the cultures . . .

And there were laboratories with doubtful objectives, such as super-habit-forming drugs like the Blues, and biologic weapons.

Essential to underground medicine are the blade runners, who transfer the actual drugs, instruments and equipment from the suppliers to the clients and doctors and underground clinics.

Some of the underground laboratories are well funded and staffed, and even the lower city grapevine does not know exactly what they are doing. Probably they are working on selective plagues and genetic engineering. There is talk of a "final solution to the problem of the sterile drones," and of blueprints for a race of supermen.

Every underground doctor needs a blade runner, since possession of illegal surgical instruments and drugs is a felony for a doctor, as evidence of illegal practice, but a misdemeanor for a private citizen. Also, the blade runners know every tunnel, alley, canal, slide, bridge and catwalk in the intricate maze of the lower city. Most of the blade runners are boys in their teens, and as minors, treated leniently by the courts when they are apprehended. Blade runners keep the underground doctors in business.

The Blade Runner

Flash of nude boy with Mercury sandals and a doctor's satchel. A boy is seen running through the streets of Lower Manhattan, dodging from one doorway to another as the credits come on. Blowing snow . . . dogs bark from the windows of derelict buildings. The boy is leaning into the wind, snow in his face. He collapses for a moment, leaning against a tree. He passes a vacant lot with frozen corn shucks. As he runs, the weather gets milder.

Frogs jump into a pothole, weeds and bushes grow up through undergrowth and gulleys full of branches. He is clearly running from something now. Sound of a chain-saw behind him. He stumbles and falls and turns scream-ing as a tree falls on him in a cloud of sawdust.

He sits up in bed, naked to the waist, a young male figure beside him in the dim dawn. Outside, the sound of a motorcycle revving up. He slides out of bed in his shorts, eyes narrow and wary as he parts the blinds and peeks out. Wan sunlight on the pale young face. Police helicopter overhead. Motorcycle takes off and rounds corner in a flurry of snow. He turns from the window, sniffing, and begins examining the room in a methodi-cal manner. He finds it behind a radiator: a short metal-lic stalk emerging like a periscope from the floorboards. At the end of the stalk, a glistening crystal bead. There is a little pile of sawdust beside the device. Flash of erect penis with a glistening bead of lubricant.

Sleepy young voice: "What is it Billy?"

Billy puts a finger to his lips. He makes a motion of looking through a telescope and wiggles his ears. The other boy throws him a towel from the bed and he drops it over the bug. He stalks back to the bed, his shorts sticking out at the fly. He stops at the foot of the bed and pulls his shorts down, and his dick flicks out like a switch-blade as Billy clicks his tongue. He kicks his shorts over his shoulder and stands there, shaking his hands above his head as if acknowledging the applause of a vast crowd. Roberts has thrown back the sheet and is sprawled naked with a hardon, one foot sideways on the floor showing the dirty sole. They look at each other and their throbbing phalluses pick up the same rhythm—throb throb throb—heartbeats like drums in the dark room. Flash of signal drums and bleeping heart beat recorders. Billy does a slow-motion pratfall, legs in the air, applauding with his feet as Roberts pivots between his legs and they do a slow-motion underwater act, Billy squirming like a clam, flushing pink and purple and iridescent as the radiator starts gurgling and trilling and thumping like a copulating dinosaur and they ride the radiator sound-effects to a chorus of tremendous thumps that shake the old building to its foundation.

Rumble of falling masonry outside.

Speed-up dress scene. Outside, a section of the building has collapsed, blocking the street. As they skirt the rubble, a pack of wild dogs rounds the corner. Billy holds up his hand, palm out, and the dogs are deflected as if they have hit a wall—they slide sideways, one throwing a last yipe of terror and defiance over his shoulder.

At an intersection a car full of uncouth youths whirls in front of them, one beefy boy leaning out and screaming "Fucking faggot blade runners!" Billy takes a quick look around. A truck is coming fast. Light changing. He yells....

"Get out of that car you yellow cock-sucker...."

Brakes slam on—truck's horn—truck plows into the back of the car, throwing people out of doors, shoes flying across the street as the gas tank explodes. The two boys look at each other, showing their teeth like wild dogs....

They pick their way through a maze of derelict buildings and open a door with a key. This is the blade runner's coop. It is a large bare room with long tables.

The coop walls are covered with paintings, drawings, cartoons and photographs, mostly the work of anonymous artists. There are pieces stolen from museums or private collections during the riots: *Custer's Last Stand, The Swimming Hole*, blowups of old photos like *Water Rats, Stern Reality*, photos by Baron von Gloeden, photos of New York in the 19th and early 20th centuries. These pictures convey most of the background material.

Life-size picture of naked boy with hardon, Mercury
wings on his sandals and helmet. The painting is in

garish pinks and blues, set in an elaborate gilded frame. The boy is posed against a Bosch background of burning cities:

The Blade Runner

Billy and Roberts stand in front of this picture and flip a coin to see who will fix dinner. Roberts takes two steaks out of an old icebox and starts fixing the meal over a wood stove. Billy walks around, looking at the pictures.

(Flashback shows Billy kicking drug habit, Roberts doling out the shots. Billy wakes up finally, over habit. Roberts points out the window. "Take a look Billy. You haven't seen the sky in a long time." Shot of clear blue sky and clouds from the Blade Runner picture.)

The Population Plague

Before: Cabin on a lake. Boy with a string of fish, a chipmunk peering out of his pocket, followed by a pet raccoon. After: Sleazy cabins all around the lake, taverns, juke-boxes, noisy drunks, motorboats, oil slicks, dead fish.

A series of cartoons from *The Watch Dog* show the plight of Mr. In The Middle:

Hotel room full of lobbyists and fixers. A laundry hamper in the middle of the floor.

"I represent Amalgamated Drugs."

"Hi, I'm from Health Insurance."

"Fill it up boys and we talk business...."

Headline: HEALTH ACT DEFEATED IN SENATE.

The First Heroin Clinic Opens Its Doors December 25, 1982.

A line of junkies marches in to the tune of "This is The Army Mr. Jones" and "You're a Lucky Fellow Mr. Smith." They put arms through grill for a shot.

1942 poster shows seaman with his sea bag and a grim expression.

"You bet I'm going back to sea."

Naked leper with hardon..."You bet I'm going back to Carrville."

Home Sweet Home

Idyllic shots of Carrville. Lepers lounge, smoking opium and pot. They are serviced by a mobile heroin clinic.

Strange Rites...Nude dances in front of the Gator Goat God...Mardi Gras in Carrville.

"IS THIS WHAT WE PAY TAXES FOR?"

One big happy welfare family . . . "Two boys on heroin maintenance" et cetera.

Mr. In The Middle with shingles goes to doctor . . . .

"*Codeine?*" Certainly not. I don't have that kind of practice. I'm writing a prescription for Whitefield's ointment. That will be fifty dollars."

Reverend Parcival orating...

Graffiti: Kill all niggers, spics, dagos, queers, and Jews....

Devil's Diary circulates. Diagrams show how to make cyanide and crushed glass bombs, nerve gas, botulism.

Blacks walk out of store with shopping bags of bug spray. The clerks look at each other...."I guess them niggers has a lot of bugs."

August 6, 1984... *The Health Act Riots... Seige of St. Vincent's... The March on Harlem General...*

Rioters release zoo animals. They dump fish from aquariums into the rivers.

The Call to Arms in Carrville

Lepers sing: "Didn't I build that cabin. (Prefabricated house...)

Didn't I plant that corn. (Poppies, Marijuana...)

A boat full of drunken vigilantes ambushed with poison darts from blowguns...

Spreading Hansen Around... A crate of leprous armadillos is released....

The National Health Act song and dance number...

The Longevity Drug... German doctor throws up his hands: "Ach Gott they will so multiply their arsen holes into the sea."

Professor Heinz addressing a class... "The conclusion seems unmistakeable. The medical miracles of the 20th century, by destroying natural immunity, result in more illness rather than less... deadly outbreak of adult diptheria in the early 1990's.... And still more alarming the incidence of hereditary degenerative diseases..... Where can this proliferation of recessive genes end?"

Einstein writes M into E on blackboard.

Heinz writes formula on blackboard.

Hiroshima.

The Health Act Amendment.

"In plain English, sterilization is now the price for any medical care."

Underground Medicine . . . Doctors operating by candlelight. Improvised respirators, artificial kidneys, iron lungs, heart pacemakers.

Clandestine Laboratories . . . Mad scientist: "With this culture we can rule the world!"

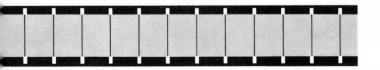

Each picture has a run of live film. They come alive as Billy looks at them. Roberts serves steaks, french fries and flapjacks with beer. Billy eats ravenously.

"Got the chucks."

In another room an accident victim is being kept alive by an improvised respirator. Signal drums pass the message along to a telephone to Billy's doc. Message passed back.

Billy and Roberts go to Parrot's supply house to get the materials necessary for a transplant operation. Dogs snarling up through subway grates. Patrol car passes. They duck into doorway and pretend to look for a name.

"What you white mothers doing here?"

"Just dodging a car."

Two black youths behind them blocking door.

"You holding?"

Roberts gives them a vial of heroin tablets. They let the runners pass.

The transplant operation is performed in a subway operating room by a delco plant. The delco is heard throughout this scene, sometimes sputtering ominously as the lights dim. All the equipment is homemade, requiring continual readjustment and tinkering. Billy goes to fetch The Hand, best operating assistant in the industry. He finds him in his pad in a converted truck, lighting matches across the room with a small homemade pistol. The Hand is a Blues addict. The Blues is a metallic variation on heroin, so named because of the bluish tinge imparted to the face. Blue is twenty times stronger than heroin. The Hand picks up his instrument case and scoops up his familiar, a black Siamese with bright blue eyes.

In the operating room the doctor is preparing himself for the operation. He drinks some hashish extract and takes a shot of morphine.

"Where's that fucking anesthetist?"

The anesthetist reels in dead drunk.

"He's shit drunk. You'll have to take over Billy."

"Who's drunk?" The anesthetist reels against the operating table. Doc has his back to him, filling a syringe with sodium pentathol.

"You're drunk. You're fired. Get out."

"You're nothing but a bunch of lousy fucking faggots!" screams the anesthetist.... "Yeah and I got news for—"

Doc turns and shoots the contents of the syringe into his open mouth.

"Shut up you gotta big mouth."

The anesthetist swallows, gurgles, coughs, sways and collapses.

"Get him out of here."

They set to work. The Hand is steady as a rock, quick and deft. Another patient is wheeled in. One doctor has a dog on a lead. The Hand's cat leaps up onto the operating table spitting, then up on top of Doc's head.

"Get that fucking dog out of here!" Doc screams. The dog is led out barking. Now other doctors come in. Scene like a Marx Brothers comedy. Stretchers, double bunks, hammocks, one patient is lashed to a post like a two-penny upright. People tripping over the wires, shooting up, making coffee, eating sandwiches, gesticulating with bloody scalpels, exchanging advice.

A doctor looks over his shoulder drinking beer from a can.... "I'd do a renal shunt if I were you."

"I can't be expected to work under such conditions," Doc says. The Hand shows him a key. They ease the stretcher out past a number of cases waiting to get in, doctors dozing, some operating by flashlights. They have a key to what had been an employee's lavatory. They try to slide the patient in without attracting notice, but another operating team almost shoves their way in. Finally they get the door closed and locked. The excluded team bangs on the door with a pipe screaming "Open the door you sons of bitches!"

"Shut up, you'll give my patient an engram...." Doc screams back. Finally the pounding stops. They get the appliances plugged in and go to work. Scene of intense concentration... The operation is finished. Faces dim and ghostly in the dawn light through a wire-glass skylight...

From this point on there are two story lines that can run alternately or on two screens. The story that we have been following up to this point becomes increasingly bizarre, dreamlike and episodic. The other story, played out in linear future set, is real and logical within the limited framework. (This is taken from the book, *The Bladerunner*).

Billy is dozing after the operation.

First sequence of dream and discovery of the bug is now repeated, except that Billy is alone in the apartment which is now jerry-built, thin walls, noise from adjoining apartments. The halls are crowded. He steps out into the streets of a teeming sordid slum, police helicopters overhead.

Billy wakes up back in the subway operating room, dim dawn through the skylight. Doc is washing his hands at a rusty tap. The Hand is shooting up. Roberts is making coffee. They are carrying the patient out on a stretcher through vegetable stalls and shoppers, down to a lower level where the tunnels are flooded, forming canals. The patient is loaded into a gondola. Roberts and Billy at the oars bellow out "Santa Lucia". They pass subway stations where boats are moored. Early morning shoppers pick over fish in dimly lit stalls. Patient is delivered to private ambulance. The chauffeur pays Doc off, and he fades into the morning shadows furtive and seedy as an old junky.

"Few more calls to make."

Billy is back in the crowded slum. He goes into Lazy Louie's, a blade runner hangout. Roberts, sitting at a table, nods curtly. Billy sits alone at another table. The waiter gives him a message.

Doc and Billy go upstairs in an old hotel. Room 18 on the top floor. They go in. Billy sniffs. Boy on bed with scarlet rash. Girlfriend reading comic books. Doc makes a cursory examination, yawning. Leaves some antibiotics. Doc and billy leave....

On the stairs Billy says "What is it Doc?"

"Looks like scarlet fever."

"Funny smell in the room."

"Oh uh incense maybe."

"He stinks like a diseased robot. Sorta rotten ozone smell."

"You got a nose like a hound Billy."

They are standing in front of a Chinese butcher shop with dressed dogs hanging on hooks in the window. Doc is looking through his pockets. A young leper in medieval leather jerkin with bells sewed on passes a greasy hat. Doc drops a coin in without looking at him. He finds the address.

Up stairs. Chinese boy, same symptoms, same rash. Same smell. Doc notices the smell this time....

As they step into the street Billy looks around....

"Run Doc it's a trap!"

Police erupt from a subway station. Doc runs down alleyway and escapes. Billy throws the satchel into a manhole where a cop who is climbing out catches it. He is booked in the old Police Headquarters at 100 Center Street. Sitting in grimy precinct room, the satchel on the table in front of him. Bored cops...

"He found it in an ash can."

"That's right," says Billy.

"He says that's right."

"And the doctor he was with...."

"He never saw him before."

"That's right," says Billy.

A cop is making a phone call. Billy dozes off....

He is back in Lazy Louie's, at the phone. Crowded buses and subways. Billy picks up tonsil instruments and medicine for an operation. Picks up Doc at the hospital. Riot of the Naturals outside. Billy helps Doc get away. Operation in kitchen. (Section from *Bladerunner* book).

Another call. Boy of sixteen plainly critical. Doc gives antibiotics and nursing instructions. As they walk down the stairs Doc says, "If I didn't know it was impossible, I'd say that was a case of smallpox with hepatic involvement...."

As they step into the street..."Run Doc it's a trap!"

Police grab Billy with the satchel. Billy in room which is more modern and clinical than the 100 Center Street room.

Billy wakes up at Center Street to see a man opening a briefcase.

"I'm from Public Health, Billy. Like to tell me about it?"

"About what?"

"Oh weeelll, Doctor Bradwell for a start...."

"Never heard of him."

"All right...all right..." The bureaucrat is leafing through papers.

Room changes and now contains a number of people, ticker tape machines, telephones, TV screens. These are highly-placed officials, bored and cynical. One is doing a crossword puzzle. Two are sniffing coke. On the TV screen we see flashes of the blade runners' coop; of Billy, Doc, and the operation. The room is reminiscent of the blade runners' coop except for the screens and the instrument panels, graphs and formulas on the wall instead of pictures. The bureaucrat is leafing through papers. He points to a graph on the wall.

"Now look at these cancer statistics. We are dealing here not just with an increase in cancer but with an increase in *susceptibility* to cancer...a breakdown in the immunity system. Why does a cancer or any virus take a certain length of time to develop? Immunity. Remove the immunity factor, and virus processes can be accelerated. Breed could land by killing or weakening cancer antibodies on a foam runway...."

"Just what are you getting at B.J.?" says a bored technician who is paring his nails.

"Just this. The virus process can be...." Nails fall in a blur of speed, speed-up yawns and coke sniffing, crossword puzzles and records....Figures on screen rushing about, old 1920 speed-up chase scene...

"Speeded up...." On screen a man drinks well water, turns yellow, mahogany, green, black, and dies.

"Accelerated hepatitis..."

Dog bites man, who falls down frothing and convulsing.

"Accelerated rabies..."

Patient in doctor's office..."Doctor I notice a little swelling this morning." He takes off his shirt to show a lump big as a baseball on his stomach, pulsing and swelling....

"Accelerated cancer..."

Doctor on phone. "Get me surgery God damn it.... Hurry or I'll have to operate with a fire axe...."

"Nature, gentlemen, imitates art. A.C. will soon be pandemic."

"How long can we keep this under wraps Doc?"

"Not long. A week at most. It's escalating geomet-

rically, like—" He presses button, and topping forest
fires appear on screen.

Back to Billy, who is lighting a cigarette....

"You can go now Billy."

Billy leaves and appears on screen in control room.

Scene shifts to another control room, much like the others. We gather oblique conversation that this is the other team.

"What about the A.C.?"

"It'll hit hardest in the middle: the sterile drones."

"The cucumbers are not committing hari kari. Something wrong here...."

Back to CIA room. "The essence of cancer is *repitition*—a cell repeating itself like an old joke. I'm a liver a liver a liver a liver...Yes an old joke with a halflife of five hundred thousand years...."

Cancer ward...Each patient is repeating an old joke over and over, like old records stuck in the same old groove....

"Who put the sand in the spinach...Ha ha ha. Who put the sand in the spinach...."

"Don't ever get rid of that cow...."

"What do you think I am, a horse?"

"We are now dickering over the price...."

"You taught me what a little is, now I'm dickering for a lot...."

"That one's on me baby."

"And who were you?"

"You know what I want, take it off and throw it up here...."

Each one round and round and round as the tumors grow and plop onto the floor. A nurse comes in and screams.

Cut back to control room. "We're hatching out all over comrades." They toast each other with insect claws.

"Blame it on the niggers."

The niggers is hatching out of us," screams the rednecks and hardhats and Southern lawmen.

"Wir hatchen juden aus!" screams a Nazi leader.

Chinese hatch out with meat cleavers....

"Fluck you. Fluck you. Fluck you."

CANCER DOCTOR ADMITS SPACE BEING HATCHING FROM TUMORS.

"Space niggers!"

"Space whities!"

Scream crazed ethnics on street corners. It's a shambles, a *sauve qui peut*. The space beings look different to everyone and are a state of mind, a possession of human bodies and minds, rather than separate entities. Everywhere they spread hate and fear and division.

Cut to control room of anti-cancer headquarters....

"Well, set a virus to catch a virus...."

Scene in coop. The boy who was diagnosed by Doc as scarlet fever collapses with nipples of flesh growing all over him like exotic plants. This is Virus B-23, the virus of biologic mutation. Nobody can have 23 and cancer at the same time. This is the vaccine against Accelerated Cancer which must be released on a mass scale. Billy and the blade runners will release it....

Back to the other story line. The health authorities now recognize that a catastrophic epidemic of smallpox, against which old-style vaccine is ineffective, has broken out. It is up to underground medicine, and especially the blade runners, to carry the message that anyone with smallpox can be treated in a hospital without submitting to *HAA*.

A new virus antibiotic has just been developed and is not yet on the underground market. Billy, who has contracted pneumonia, is spreading the word to suspicious dealers and runners who think he is a shill from Health Control.

Billy in the subways. The canals have resulted in

the lower tunnels being flooded. Much of the produce of New York is conveyed here on boats, and on the upper level in steam- and hand-propelled cars. The Stations are now markets lit by skylights of wired glass letting in a dim grey light fading into the inky blackness of unlighted tunnels and canals. Here light is a precious resource, to be hoarded and guarded. A man lights his flash for a moment and shadows close in from all sides. He pulls his pistol: "Keep away from my light, you creeps."

The delco gangs sell a bootleg electrical service from subway delco systems. They are in competition, and gang warfare is constant. Often the lower city is without any light service. Lever flash lights are a prized possession and sell for $200.

Billy is making his way down through the vegetable stalls and flower markets. A pack of wild dogs leaps from a dark tunnel. Billy uses a sonic pistol that reduces them to infantile cowardice, cringing and pissing on themselves. The blade runners sprint past them and hail a gondola. They give an address.

"This is my old heroin dealer. Into *pop* now, I hear."

Carbide lamp on the prow of the gondola. Alligators slide out from subway stations in the dark water... shark fins. A glimmer of light ahead where a torch lights a private jetty. The dealer has hewn out a bunker, running a number of change rooms and lavatories together.

He shakes his head sadly with a terrible Italian smile.... "If it was heroin or the Blues or *pop* even...But 23—not me. Do yourself one favor and beat it."

They push on. They are armed with a number of sophisticated weapons: sonic guns and small flame-throwers for the dogs, a crushed glass and sodium cyanide pistol for short-range heavy duty, a silencered 20-shot nail gun, knives and cyanide injectors for hand-to-hand fighting.

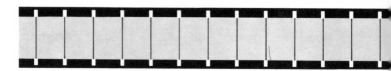

Back to the other story line. Cold with a biting wind, teeth chattering uncontrollably, the cough so painful he has to lean against a lamp post from time to time. Half the time he is in a stupor, half out on his feet... stairways, alleys and crowded streets flashing by in a blurred succession. At one place someone hurled him down a flight of stairs. Later someone was feeding him a warm watery soup that made him gag and cough.

Mad vigilantes with hangman's nooses and shotguns in canoes and rafts stalk the underground tunnels, the swamps and canals. There are also the dreaded tunnel pirates, the warring delco gangs, and all the underground scavengers. Some of these can only crawl, but they will hamstring you with wire-cutters set in their radioactive glowing stumps.... Others are hit-and-run, grabbing a weapon, a flashlight, a camera and darting back into the tunnels and warrens and dens they have carved out over the years.

Billy, Roberts and The Hand now have the most dangerous job in the trade: running vaccine in the form of a weakened virus strain to be released on an epidemic scale. Often there are miscalculations, and some of the vaccines have almost as high a mortality rate as the disease itself. In this case they are admittedly shooting for a pretty narrow margin. The desperate cancer agents will now resort to any means to stop the spread of B-23. The ignorant and bigoted natives have been aroused to a frenzy. To be caught with the vaccine means a horrible death at the hands of the mobs.

Virus B-23, the virus of biologic mutation, after lying dormant for 23,000 years in two crystal skulls, is rediscovered by Doktor Unruh von Steinplatz. He calls it Unruh's Disease. U.D. is characterized by an itching burning erogenous rash in the genitals and surrounding areas, accompanied by an uncontrollable sexual frenzy. U.D. victims undergo bizarre changes in pigmentation during intercourse, and these changes are genetically conveyed.

U.D. was extracted by the Herr Doktor by exposing the crystal skulls to D.O.R.—Deadly Orgone Radiation—in a highly magnetized iron pyramid. This energy, then projected onto copulating couples, produces the syndrome of U.D. No one can have U.D. and cancer at the same time. Admittedly U.D. has a high mortality rate, particularly in the elderly or in those whose character structure is rigid and resistant to change. On the other hand, U.D. is welcomed by adventurous youth.

Posters and placards:

    FREEDOM TO MUTATE

    ORGONE ENERGY NOT RADIATION

    U.D. NOT CANCER

The decision to release U.D. on a mass scale to combat the cancer epidemic caused a furor when it leaked to the press...lynch mobs, burning cities....

"Well now it never would have leaked out like that in front of decent people except for some technical hang-ups. We had just two of these artifacts, the crystal skulls, containing the virus code made 23,000 years ago in an area that is now the Gobi desert and was at that time the site of an advanced civilization which was wiped out by the virus.

"So we split the project into Team A and Team B. We found that neither A nor B alone was able to reproduce itself and cause secondary infection. Each strain alone was sterile as a mule, and we needed a virgin soil epidemic to stem the foam runway of flash cancer. It was only by uniting the two strains that the virus could reproduce and do its work. So Team A with the A strain and Team B with the B strain are trying to join up all over Manhattan and Greater New York City, making a different meet every day.

Lynch mobs, false police, real police, agents official and self-appointed, guardians, minute men, watch dogs, the veterans of S.O.C., are all out to stop U.D. Chases and shoot-downs. The whole underground is supporting the teams. The A Team is rescued by hang-glider boys who swoop down from the World Trade Center, their Venus machine guns farting like a herd of stallions.

"Meet at T.E....."

"That's Grand Central—let's go."

At first they slide along unnoticed. But as they approach Grand Central, in an area of small shops, suddenly everyone sees them. Everywhere they look, a suspicious hostile eye peering out of a shop window, turning to look after them, closing in behind them, muttering, rising up in their path—faces of sulphurous hate closing in on all sides, others massed behind them....

"You lousy plague runners...."

"Stop right there...."

"You carrying nigger eggs?"

"What we carry is our business. Out of the way."

A bulky hardhat steps in front of Roberts and reaches for a gun in his belt. Roberts brings out his spring knife, it snaps forward on a heavy spring from a tube into the man's stomach. He grunts and doubles over as Roberts pulls the knife free, whipping it back and forth. The front ranks fall backwards into those behind them. A shotgun blast shatters a shop window by The Hand's head, spattering his face with red dots. His silencered nail gun is out: *sput sput sput.* Billy draws his cyanide and crushed glass pistol and blasts a hole in the crowd. The boys sprint through.

The other team is closing in from the other side. The mob scatters. The two teams rush together.

"I'm AAAAAAAA! "

"I'm BBBBBBB!"

Both teams are the same actors now, wearing old style gym clothes with "A" or "B" on the shirt front. They embrace in a blur of snow, confetti and streamers—cheering crowds, VJ Day, VE Day, the Armistice. Station

is moving back in time—1914 passengers, long train
whistles...

Scene from *Bladerunner* book: Billy in the Silver Dollar
Bar. Turn of the century decorations, *Custer's Last Stand*
over the bar. The patrons wear 1914 clothes. Billy con-
tacts Roberts, who is suspicious. Billy explains that an
epidemic of smallpox is underway. He has some virus
antibiotic pills. But most victims will have to go to the
hospital. No questions will be asked. He gives Roberts a
package of the pills.

The Naturists—who look like turn-of-the-century
cranks, a lynch mob out to get the Mormons—are moving down the bar, staring at the boys with wild uncouth
faces. A huge one stands in front of Roberts.

"Hold it bud. What's in the package?"

"That's my business."

"Any lousy blade runner with bootleg medical supplies is my business. Hand it over."

Roberts hits the man in the midriff with his fist,
then brings a hammer fist to the side of his neck. Roberts

and his two friends make the door. Billy is on his feet. He sidesteps one man, catches another with a nose chop. Three others stand between him and the door. He trips one, uses a bar stool as a pivot to swing past the other two. Someone puts out a leg—he trips and falls, turning as he goes down. (This shot is identical with dream shot as he trips, falls and turns to face pursuer.) Someone grabs for him. He twists free, leaving his sweater, and runs out the door in shirtsleeves.

Turn-of-the-century streets, potholes frozen over, empty warehouses, broken windows, railroad tracks at the end of the street. Three burly Naturists run after him and grab him. He fights viciously with feet, knees and elbows. One pulls a knife. Lights from old army car. The men run....

"Don't run Billy. It's me, Doc."

Billy sways and falls forward. Train whistle.

Billy wakes up in the hospital. Doc tells him he came near dying of pneumonia and exposure. He and the other blade runners are now heroes of the Epidemic.

"What epidemic?"

"Why the smallpox epidemic of course. It's under control now."

"Doc, what's the date?"

"January 18th."

"The whole date Doc."

"January 18th, 1914."

Doc leaves. Billy goes to the window and looks out. A clear night, stars in the sky over 1914 Manhattan skyline. (This is to be prepared by researching and selecting what buildings were in the skyline at that time.) Beginning dream sequence is repeated. Billy is running and dodging through shabby streets with a package under his arm. He is leaning into windblown snow and icy wind in a thin sweater coughing, staggering, stopping in doorways to get his breath. Dogs snarl up through subway gratings. The Naturists bar his way. Fight in bar and shoot-out in Grand Central. The Naturists who have pursued him into the street scatter as Doc arrives in 1914 army car. Mob scatters in Grand Central as the other team opens up from behind them. Snow blurs into confetti, streamers, cheering crowds in Times Square. Advertisement shows animated figure in lights running across the Manhattan skyline.

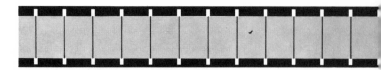

The Blade Runner

    Flashback to starlit sky over 1914 skyline as seen from the hospital window....